There's Going
to be a baby

*With love to
Klara and Emil*
H. O.

First published 2010 by Walker Books Ltd
87 Vauxhall Walk, London SE11 5HJ

This edition published 2011

2 4 6 8 10 9 7 5 3 1

Text © 2010 John Burningham
Illustrations © 2010 Helen Oxenbury

The right of John Burningham and Helen Oxenbury
to be identified as author and illustrator respectively of this work
has been asserted by them in accordance with the
Copyright, Designs and Patents Act 1988

This book has been typeset in Polymer

Printed in China

British Library Cataloguing in Publication Data:
a catalogue record for this book is available from the British Library

ISBN 978-1-4063-3108-0

www.walker.co.uk

WALKER BOOKS
AND SUBSIDIARIES
LONDON · BOSTON · SYDNEY · AUCKLAND

There's Going To Be A Baby

John Burningham
Helen Oxenbury

There's going to be a baby.

When is the baby going to come?

The baby will arrive when it's ready, in the autumn, when the leaves are turning brown and falling.

What will we call the baby?

If it's a little girl I'd like to call it Susan or Josephine or perhaps Jennifer.

I hope it's a boy, so we can play together, boys' games, and I think it should be called Peter or Spiderman.

What will the baby do?

Maybe the baby
will work in the
kitchen and
perhaps be
a chef.

I don't think
I'd eat anything
that was made
by the baby.

Maybe the baby
will grow up to
be an artist and
paint lovely
pictures.

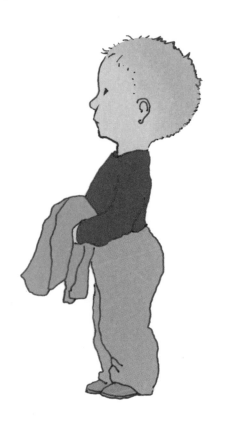

If the baby is
an artist, don't let it
paint pictures in our
house. It will make
a terrible mess
everywhere.

Perhaps the baby will be a gardener and make things grow.

When the baby's bigger, it can play with me.

Mummy, can't you
tell the baby to go away?
We don't really need
the baby, do we?

I wonder if the baby will work here in the zoo one day, looking after the animals.

Then the baby might get eaten by a tiger.

I wonder if the baby will be a sailor and take us out in a boat.

We could sail round the world, but I think I should be the captain.

Perhaps the baby
will work here
in the bank when
it is older.

Well, that would
be very good.
Then it could
give me lots
of money.

Mrs Anderson's baby was sick
all over their new carpet.

They always need people
to work in the park,
so that is something
the baby could do
later on.

I don't think the
baby could ever
collect up all
these leaves.

The baby could
be a doctor or
a nurse when it
grows up.

I hope the baby
doesn't look
after me if
I'm ill.

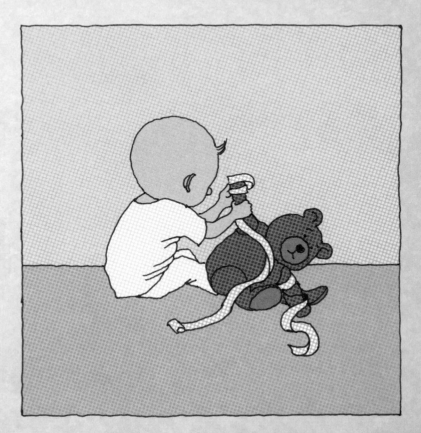

When is the baby coming, Mummy?
I want to see the baby.

It won't be long now.
The baby is being as quick as it can.

Grandad, we're going to
see the baby now.
Maybe it will be Susan or Peter.
Maybe it will be good at cooking
and it will sail on the seven seas
and work in the garden or
the zoo or the bank.

Grandad,
the baby will
be our baby.
We're going to
love the baby,
aren't we?